GW00859014

The wonderful tale of Giraffe the giraffe (who was also a superhero)

A story with pictures by
Jacob Prytherch

Copyright © 2015-2016 Jacob Prytherch

All rights reserved.

No copying or redistribution of this text may occur without the consent of the author.

ISBN: 1523387521
ISBN-13: 978-1523387526

For Rosie

On the grassy plains of Africa, where it gets hotter than the top of a bald man's head in the noonday sun, there lived a giraffe.

Well the truth is that there were lots of giraffes - herds of them - but we're going to look at one in particular. There she is, just at the back, having a drink from the watering hole.

Her name was Giraffe. All the other giraffes had colourful names like Peter, Eugenie, Gustav or Longshanks, but Giraffe liked the simplicity of her name. It meant she knew who she was, which was an important thing to know.

Her neck was long and her legs were bony. Her eyes were deep and dark. Poets might have called them world-weary, but really she just squinted a lot because of the brightness of the African sunshine.

You could say that Giraffe looked the same as all the other giraffes, but she knew that she was special. What made her special was her secret, a secret that she kept from all the other animals.

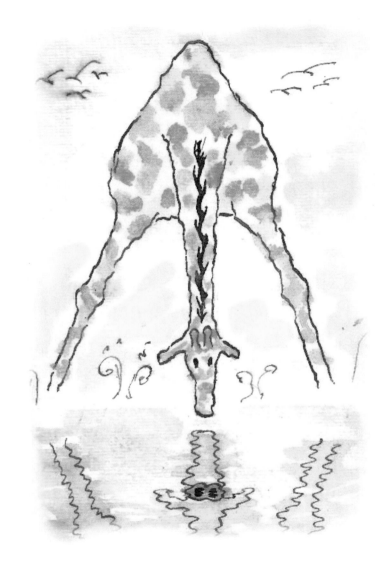

Ever since she was small, (as small as you can be when you're a giraffe), she had wanted to be a superhero.

She knew that superheroes needed costumes, but she didn't have any money (her parents never gave her any pocket money because she didn't have pockets, and they had never thought to buy her any trousers). So she decided to get a job delivering joke books to hyenas.

When she had finally saved up enough money she looked through a catalogue and chose a costume made of purple and yellow cloth. It had a large letter G on the front, just under the nape of her neck (which was quite prominent on a giraffe). The G stood for giraffe. They even had a giraffe modelling it.

The other thing that a superhero needs is a special power. She didn't have any special powers, as far as she knew, but she was sure that they would come in time. Even though giraffes weren't very original they made up for it by being natural optimists.

When her parcel arrived she tore off the wrapping and put the costume on straight away, without even looking in the mirror to see if it was straight. After all, she knew that trouble didn't wait for superheroes to get ready before it became troublesome. It was always troublesome. So she started her new career with slightly ruffled socks.

As she marched through the tall grass of the savannah - being careful not to squash any meerkats - she wondered what the best way to find trouble was. She didn't have a telephone and received very few letters generally, so she needed to do something else. She needed to be extra attentive, that was the key.

She lifted her ears as high as she could. and almost immediately she heard a trumpeting to her right. And what is more, it was a particularly troubled trumpeting...

"This sounds like a job for me, Giraffe!" thought Giraffe.

She galloped off at her fastest speed, a creditable fifty kilometres per hour.

She arrived (very quickly) at the site of what can only be described as pandemonium, but only if you didn't really know what the word meant. It was more of a kerfuffle.

Three elephants were jostling together at the waterhole. Their trunks were tangling and their bottoms were wiggling. Some water splashed onto the dry earth and made it a little bit muddy.

"Those poor elephants. This really is too much!" thought Giraffe.

She galloped over to the watering hole. The elephants stopped drinking and looked at her. Then they looked at each other. Then they looked at her again.

She let the wind ripple her cape a little.

"Don't worry!" said Giraffe.

"Alright." said Lewis, the largest of the elephants.

"Your troubles are over!" added Giraffe.

"Wonderful." replied Lewis. "Good to know. What troubles?"

"If you stand in a triangle," said Giraffe. ignoring the silly question, "then you can all drink comfortably without touching bottoms."

The elephants shuffled to their positions, just as Giraffe had suggested. They each took a sip. Their bottoms swung freely, touching nothing but air.

"Well, this is good." said Lewis.

"It is?" grinned Giraffe.

"Very comfortable."

"My first heroic deed!" said Giraffe. "I may have found my superpower!"

"Superpower?" asked Lewis. "I wouldn't say that. It was clever, most definitely, but moving elephants' bottoms isn't very super."

"Oh," said Giraffe.

"It's still very good," said Lewis. "Chin up."

"I'm Giraffe, my chin is always up," said Giraffe, walking away. "And I will find my superpower!"

She didn't have to wait long for more trouble as she soon heard a weeping from the banks of the river. She found a little hippopotamus, crying his tiny eyes out.

"What's the matter, little one?" asked Giraffe.

"My mummy," said the little hippopotamus. "I can't find her."

"Hold my tail," said Giraffe. "I'll find her!"

"How?" asked the little hippopotamus.

"Using my superpowers!"

"What superpowers?"

"I'm not sure yet..."

Giraffe took a deep breath and started walking. The bank was muddy and crowded. There were flamingos and crocodiles and quite a large number of hippopotamuses washing themselves.

"How will we find my mummy?" asked the little hippopotamus.

Giraffe stretched her neck up as high as she could and looked around. She knew what she was looking for and she soon saw it. A large motherpotamus named Babette was looking around with tears in her eyes. Giraffe gently pulled the little hippopotamus towards her.

"Mummy!" cried the little hippopotamus with joy.

"Spencer!" cried Babette.

Giraffe was very happy to see the joy on the little hippopotamus' face, who she now knew was called Spencer.

"Mummy, a superhero saved me!" said Spencer.

Babette the motherpotamus smiled at Giraffe, showing her huge round teeth. "Thank you so much! How can we ever repay you?"

"No need," said Giraffe, glowing with pride. "Finally knowing my superpower is reward enough."

Babette looked up at her. "What power?"

"Well," said Giraffe. "finding. The finding of someone... who was sad. Sad-finding. And helping a little hippopotamus."

Babette bit her rubbery lip. "I'm sorry, but I don't think that's a super power. It's very kind, but it's not super."

Giraffe felt like a balloon that had been sat on. She sniffed. "Oh."

"Don't worry, I'm sure you'll find your power soon," said Spencer.

Giraffe turned and walked away.

"Stand tall!" called Babette.

"I always do," mumbled Giraffe.

Giraffe didn't know what to do. She'd tried to find her superpower twice, but all she found was that she was clever and kind, which was nice, but it wasn't *super*.

"Maybe I'll never find my superpower," she thought as she stared up at the clouds. "Maybe I don't have one. Maybe..."

She stopped. She realised she was walking under a tree and it looked like a lion was stuck in it. His arms were dangling down in despair. Well, it could have been tiredness, but it looked like despair.

"How horrible," thought Giraffe. "Look at the fear in his eyes."

She knew she needed to act quickly. Her destiny was calling.

Giraffe pushed her neck out and pressed it to the lion's paw.

"Don't worry," said Giraffe. "I'll save you!"

The lion yawned a big yawn - with lots of teeth - and looked down at the thing that was pressed against his paw.

"I'm sorry?"

"No need to apologise," said Giraffe briskly. "Let's just get you to safety."

The lion, who was called Ashwell, yawned again.

"Well, I do need to go hunting at some point. Now's as good a time as any I suppose."

Ashwell the lion started to wriggle his body down Giraffe's neck. His fur was all fluffy and his paws tickled Giraffe's throat, but she stayed strong until the lion was on the ground.

"Thank you. Most kind," said Ashwell.

Giraffe gave a watery smile.

"I was wondering..." she started, before swallowing nervously. Her words caught in her long, long throat. "I was wondering if you'd say that was a super power?"

"What? That neck? Your long giraffe's neck?" asked Ashwell.

Giraffe nodded.

Ashwell shrugged his furry shoulders. "Well. I couldn't have done it. so sure." he said. "Why not?"

"You mean it?" asked Giraffe.

"Yeah," said Ashwell. He stretched out on the grass.
"You're a superhero."

Giraffe beamed. She jumped for joy.

And — as she found out when she didn't land back on the ground — she could also fly, so she had two superpowers.

So that's good.

About the author

Jacob Prytherch is a writer but he's also a father, and he knows which is the most important (it's not the writing), so he combined the two and wrote a story for his daughter Rosie.

He hopes she will enjoy it, and that you do too.

Facebook.com/jakeprytherch
http://jakeprytherch.wix.com/main